Making a Shadow Puppet

Jonathon Phillips
Photographs by Lindsay Edwards

Contents

Goal

To make a shadow puppet theatre and a shadow puppet

Materials

You will need:

- two big pieces of black paper (300 mm × 420 mm)
- one small piece of black paper (210 mm × 297 mm)
- glue

- a white pencil
- a ruler

- scissors

- **baking paper**

- a stapler

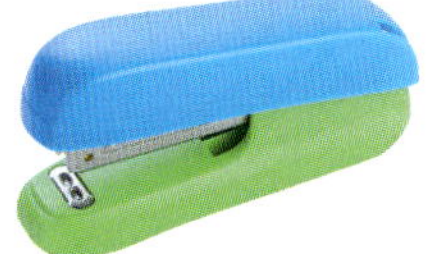

- Blu Tack

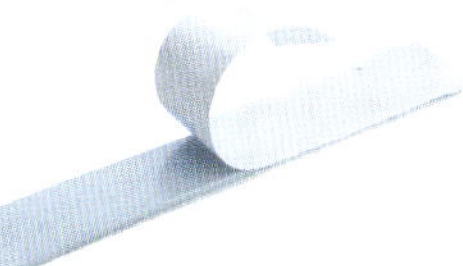

- a stick (like a chopstick)

- a **torch**.

Steps

Make the Theatre

1. Put the two big pieces of black paper on the table.

2. Put glue around the outside of the pieces of paper.

3. Then, put one piece of paper on top of the other.

Stick the pieces of paper together.

4. When the glue is dry, **fold** the paper, like this.

5. Next, draw three white lines
on the black paper with the pencil and ruler.

6. Cut along the white lines with scissors.

7. Open out the black paper.
It will look just like a window.

8. Next, cut a rectangle
out of the baking paper.
Make it a bit smaller than
the black paper.

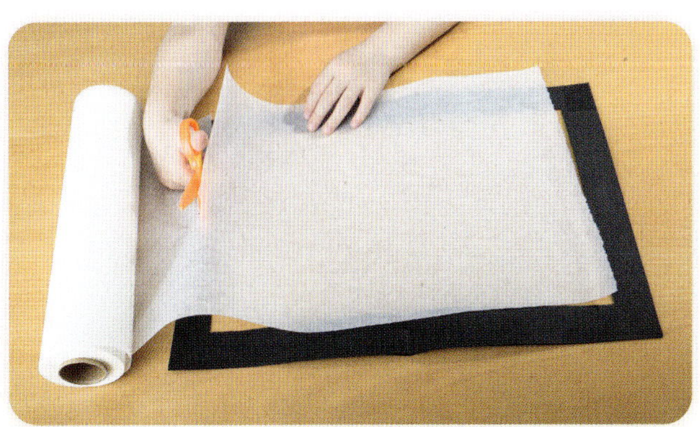

9. Staple the baking paper
to the black paper with the stapler.

10. Fold the paper again, like this.

11. Then, open it out.

This is your shadow puppet theatre.

Make the Puppet

1. Put the small piece of black paper on the table.
   Draw a funny face with the white pencil.
   Give the face two eyes and a mouth.

2. Cut out the puppet's face.
Ask a parent or teacher to help you with the eyes and mouth.

3. With the Blu Tack, stick the chopstick to the back of the puppet.
Your shadow puppet is done.

4. Next, turn off all the lights in the room.
Then, turn the torch on
and place it behind
the shadow puppet theatre.

5. Hold your puppet
near to the shadow puppet theatre.
The torch will be behind the puppet.

Move your puppet up and down
with the chopstick.

Now, you are ready
for your shadow puppet show!

Glossary

baking paper paper that light can shine through

fold to bend something over

torch a small light that you can hold in your hand

Making a Shadow Puppet

Text: Jonathon Phillips
Publisher: Eliza Webb
Editor: Vanessa Dodd
Project editor: Jarrah Moore
Project designer: James Steer
Designer: MAPG
Photographs: Lindsay Edwards
Production controller: Alice Kane
Reprint: Siew Han Ong

Acknowledgements
Back cover (background pattern): Shutterstock.com/sahua d.

PM Guided Reading
Orange Level 15

The Dinosaur Chase
A Present for Bella
That Goat Must Go!
Toby and BJ
Toby and the Big Tree
Cassie's Crutches
Gia's New School
Pterosaur's Long Flight
Tiger Cat and Tabby Cat
Guinea Pigs
Cats
Dogs
Making a Shadow Puppet
The Fun House
Trucks

ISBN 978 0 17 032819 7

Cengage Learning Australia
Level 5 , 80 Dorcas Street
Southbank VIC 3006
Phone: 1300 790 853
Email: aust.nelsonprimary@cengage.com

For learning solutions, visit cengage.com.au

Printed in China by 1010 Printing International Ltd
2 3 4 5 6 7 24

PM

1 2 3 4 5 6 7 8 9 10 11 12 13 14 15 16 17 18 19 20 21 22 23 24 25 26 27 28 29 30

A shadow puppet theatre can be made out of things you will find at home or school. Learn how to make a shadow puppet theatre and a funny shadow puppet!

Procedure

ISBN 978-0170328197

Leve
15